THE NOTEBOOK OF DOOM

SNAP OF THE SUPER-GOOP

by Troy Cummings

BRANCHES

SCHOLASTIC INC.

Ready for more fun with your favorite series?

EERIE ELEMENTARY by Jack Chabert, illustrated by Sam Ricks

DRAGON MASTERS by Tracey West, illustrated by Graham Howells

THE NOTEBOOK OF DOOM
by Troy Cummings

More books coming soon!

TABLE OF CONTENTS

CHAPTER 1: THE SALAMANDER REPORT   1

CHAPTER 2: GOING, GOING, GOON!   7

CHAPTER 3: TWO LATE TO CLASS   12

CHAPTER 4: STINK SAUCE   16

CHAPTER 5: LITTLE SQUIRT   23

CHAPTER 6: BLOWN AWAY   28

CHAPTER 7: NOT IT!   33

CHAPTER 8: THE FOURTH MEMBER   41

CHAPTER 9: SNOW FOOLIN'   46

CHAPTER 10: CRASH COURSE   53

CHAPTER 11: THE LAST STRIKE   56

CHAPTER 12: BLAH BLAH BLOB   62

CHAPTER 13: QUITE A STRETCH   68

CHAPTER 14: OOZE THE NEW GUY?   73

CHAPTER 15: COOK WHO'S TALKING   77

CHAPTER 16: NO BOOK OF DOOM   83

To Edie: Some people say you were just a cat. But to me, you were a member of the family—a hairball-hacking, flea-ridden, toddler-chomping, dog-chasing member of the family. R.I.P.

Thank you, Katie Carella and Liz Herzog, for shaping, molding, and sculpting my story into something awesome. And for smoothing out the lumpy parts.

Thank you, Professor Vaglia, for grading Alexander's homework.

Copyright © 2016 by Troy Cummings

Library of Congress Cataloging-in-Publication Data

Names: Cummings, Troy, author. | Cummings, Troy. Notebook of doom ; 10.
Title: Snap of the super-goop / by Troy Cummings.
Description: First edition. | New York, NY : Branches/Scholastic Inc., 2016.
  | ©2016 | Series: The Notebook of Doom ; 10 | Summary: Alexander keeps seeing monsters he has previously conquered, but every time he gets close they disappear and his friends are beginning to think he is delusional—but when one of their teachers turns into a blob of super-goop right before their eyes they realize the team is dealing with a shape-shifter, and it is after the Notebook of Doom.
Identifiers: LCCN 2015048822| ISBN 9780545864992 (pbk.) | ISBN 9780545865005 (hardcover)
Subjects: LCSH: Monsters—Juvenile fiction. | Shapeshifting—Juvenile
  fiction. | Elementary schools—Juvenile fiction. | Friendship—Juvenile
  fiction. | Horror tales. | CYAC: Monsters—Fiction. |
  Shapeshifting—Fiction. | Schools—Fiction. | Friendship—Fiction. |
  Horror stories. | GSAFD: Horror fiction.
Classification: LCC PZ7.C91494 Sn 2016 | DDC 813.6—dc23
LC record available at http://lccn.loc.gov/2015048822

10 9 8 7 6 5 4 3 2 1   16 17 18 19 20

Printed in China   38
First edition, July 2016

Book design by Liz Herzog

CHAPTER 1

THE SALAMANDER REPORT

It was way past bedtime when Alexander put down his pencil. He smiled at his drawing of a bug-eating, wall-climbing, tongue-flicking creature.

KNOCK-KNOCK! Alexander's dad stepped into the room.

"How is your homework going, kiddo?" he asked.

"All done," said Alexander, holding up his report. "I hope my teacher likes it."

"Dr. Tallow's going to *love* it!" said his dad. "Now, get some sleep!"

Alexander climbed into bed.

"Sleep tight, Al," said his dad. He turned out the lights.

Alexander thought about how much fun he'd had writing his salamander paper. He had been writing similar reports ever since moving to Stermont. But these other reports were not about animals. They were about monsters.

Alexander pulled a beat-up old notebook from beneath his pillow.

Salamanders are not really *fire monsters,* he thought. Then he opened the notebook to read about a *real* fire monster.

Alexander closed the notebook.

A flame-deer must have burned those pages when it battled the old S.S.M.P.! he thought.

S.S.M.P. stood for "Super Secret Monster Patrol." The original S.S.M.P. had created the notebook to protect Stermont from monsters. The monster patrol now had three members — Alexander and his two best friends:

SUPER SECRET MONSTER PATROL
CLUB MEMBERS

Alexander
The leader!

Nikki
Brave and clever!

Rip
Short but ~~sweet!~~
strong

And tomorrow, we might be adding a new member! Alexander thought. He smiled, and drifted off to sleep.

2 GOING, GOING, GOON!

The next morning, Alexander was running late. He double-checked his backpack to make sure he had his two most important items:

1. The monster notebook.
2. His animal report.

Then he hopped on his bike and rode to school.

Alexander coasted over to the bike rack. He set his bike lock.

February 29th, he thought. *My birthday is easy to remember!*

CLICKETY-CLICK! Alexander scrambled the numbers on his lock. Then he froze. Something wobbled around, off to his left. Something green and wiggly.

Alexander jumped. *A snake?*

SWISH! The green thing flopped beneath a hedge.

Snakes don't move like that, he thought. *Maybe it's a monster!*

School was about to start. But Alexander knew that stopping a monster was more important than being on time to class.

The green thing wriggled through the hedge. Alexander ran to the other side. His jaw dropped.

The green thing wasn't a snake. It was an arm!
The flippy, flapping arm of a balloon goon!

BALLOON GOON
Wiggly-wobbly
air-sucking monster

The goon fixed its googly eyes on Alexander.
Alexander had battled balloon goons before.
In fact, they were the first monsters he had
run into when he'd moved to Stermont.

"I thought we popped all you
goons," he said, pulling a sharp
pencil from his backpack. "We
must have missed one."

The goon bounced around the corner of the
school. Alexander ran after it.

But there was no monster behind the school. Just a huge garbage dumpster.

CLANG-CLONG! Something banged against the other side of the dumpster. Alexander snuck over. He leaped out with a battle cry.

SCRISSHHH! Alexander's pencil tore through something shiny and plastic. A garbage bag. An overstuffed garbage bag in the arms of a tall, white-haired man.

"Eep!" The white-haired man flailed his arms, flinging garbage everywhere.

"Mr. Hoarsely?!" shouted Alexander.

MR. HOARSELY

- School secretary, janitor, nurse, bus driver, and gym teacher
- Former S.S.M.P. member
- Only grown-up who can see monsters?
- HUGE fraidycat!

"I was just taking out the trash!" cried Mr. Hoarsely, pulling a banana peel off his shoulder. "Why did you attack me?"

"Sorry! I thought you were a balloon goon," Alexander said. He looked around. "Did you see one wobble this way?"

Mr. Hoarsely swallowed. "What?! N-n-no! I thought you guys destroyed every last one of those horrible things!"

"Yeah," said Alexander. "I thought so, too."

BRINNGGGGG!!

Mr. Hoarsely jumped again. "The late bell," he said. "I'll clean this up — you get to class!"

CHAPTER 3 TWO LATE TO CLASS

Alexander sprinted up the escalators. He was out of breath by the time he reached the ninth floor. He rushed into his classroom.

Alexander looked around. Students were talking, laughing, and running all over the place.

"You sure picked the right day to be late, Salamander!" someone shouted. "There's no teacher!"

Alexander turned to see Rip holding a big yellow box that said HANDS OFF!

"Dr. Tallow is even later than you are!" said Nikki, rushing over. "What kind of teacher —"

"Guys!" Alexander interrupted. He lowered his voice. "I saw a balloon goon!"

Nikki's eyes widened. "You did?! Where?"

"Behind the school," said Alexander.

"No way!" Rip said.

"Did you pop it?" Nikki asked.

"Well, no," said Alexander. "I mean, I tried to — I ran after it. But it just vanished! I ended up slashing a garbage bag instead."

"I hate to burst your bubble, Salamander," said Rip, "but balloon goons can't just disappear."

"Maybe the garbage bag *looked* like a balloon goon?" suggested Nikki.

"But —" Alexander began.

"So, Salamander," said Rip, "before you fought the garbage bag, did you finish your animal report? Bet it's not as awesome as mine!" Rip shook his yellow box.

"Yep, I finished it," said Alexander. "It was fun!"

"For *you*, maybe," said Nikki. "I had to write about crummy goldfish."

"*Pfft!* Whatever!" said Rip. "You're just jealous because Dr. Tallow likes me more than you!" He pointed to the board.

TWENTY STRIKES AND YOU'RE OUT!
NIKKI: xxxxx xxxxx xxxxx xxx
RIP: x

The door swung open. Dr. Tallow walked in.

"Sorry I'm late," she said, rubbing lotion on her hands. "I left my lotion in the car! My skin dries right up without it."

But most students didn't hear her. They were still chatting loudly.

Dr. Tallow clapped her hands.

CLAP! CLAP! CLAP-CLAP-CLAP!

The students echoed her clap back to her.

"That's better," said Dr. Tallow. She turned to Nikki, smiling. "Except for you. Your claps were a teensy bit late."

Dr. Tallow went to the board and added a nineteenth X beside Nikki's name.

Nikki tugged on her hoodie strings until only her narrowed eyes were visible.

4 STINK SAUCE

"Take your seats, dearies," said Dr. Tallow. "We'll begin our animal reports."

Alexander sat next to a girl in a bunny shirt.

"Hi, Dottie!" he said. Dottie had been around for a couple of monster battles, but she wasn't a member of the S.S.M.P. . . . at least, not yet. She gave Alexander a little wave.

"Dottie Rogers, why don't you start us off?" said Dr. Tallow.

Dottie jumped up. "Sure! But first I need something from the classroom-pet zone," she said.

Dr. Tallow led Dottie to a door at the back of the room. She punched a few numbers into a keypad, and the door swung open. Dottie stepped inside.

Alexander knew this room well. It was lined with cages that held every kind of classroom pet. Dr. Tallow taught animal lessons in there.

CLASSROOM-PET ZONE

HAMSTERS SNAKES BIRDS FISH

BUNNIES TURTLES HERMIT CRABS LIZARDS

Dottie came out cradling a white-and-brown rabbit.

"My report is about the very cutest, cuddliest, fluffiest animals of ALL: bunnies!" she said. "They're super neat — and I've got the numbers to prove it!"

"Excellent work," said Dr. Tallow. "Next up: Alexander Bopp."

Alexander gave his report. He could tell he was talking too fast, but everyone seemed interested — especially Dr. Tallow.

"Terrific," Dr. Tallow said. "I didn't know salamanders could regrow lost legs. That could sure come in handy!"

After a few more reports, it was Rip's turn.

"Ladies, gentlemen, and weenies," he said to the class. "Prepare to be blown away by the Texas horned lizard!"

He drew a spiky creature on the board.

"This desert reptile can puff itself up," said Rip. "But that's not the coolest part . . . Let's say a hungry bad-guy animal is prowling around. The Texas horned lizard can protect itself by shooting blood from its eyes!"

TEXAS HORNED LIZARD!

Students gasped.

"Yes, yes — amazing!" Rip continued. "But it gets better! The blood is mixed with stuff that makes it taste and smell super gross. Let me show you!"

Rip tore open his big box. Inside was a strange hat-and-goggles set.

"Howdy, y'all!" said Rip, strapping on the headgear. "I'm the Texas horned lizard."

Some students shifted in their seats.

"Uh-oh," Rip continued. "Here comes a hungry coyote!"

COWBOY HAT

SPIKES

GOGGLES

SQUIRT-SOAKER

HANDS OFF!

He pulled out a crude doglike drawing and set it up on the bookcase.

"Sure, Mr. Coyote, I look like a tasty snack," said Rip. "But how does THIS taste?!"

GOOSH! He squeezed his squirt-soaker, blasting the coyote with red, stinky liquid.

The coyote drooped.

"Gross!" someone shouted. "Ew! That smells *terrible*!"

"Yep!" said Rip, smiling. "That's the idea! I made it myself!"

RIP'S STINK SAUCE RECIPE

- Beet juice
- Cod liver oil
- Ketchup
- Vinegar

Stir until you almost puke.

Students were gagging from the stench of Rip's stink sauce.

"Very creative, Rip dear," said Dr. Tallow. She was pinching her nose so hard it looked sort of squished. "Everyone, head down to lunch while I open some windows. We'll finish the reports tomorrow."

CHAPTER 5 LITTLE SQUIRT

🍴 CAFETERIA →

Ｈow can we eat when we're still gagging from Rip's stink sauce?" said Alexander as his class made its way down to the cafeteria.

"That sauce smelled pretty tasty to me!" said Nikki.

Rip grinned. "I knew you'd say that, you crazy jampire."

Nikki was secretly a monster — a good monster called a jampire. She could see in the dark, and she loved anything red and juicy.

"Think fast!" Rip added. He tossed Nikki a bag of his leftover stink sauce. She smiled. Then she read the lunch menu, and smiled a little less.

Alexander, Rip, and Nikki filled their trays. They joined Dottie at an empty table.

"Hi, guys!" Dottie said. "Rip, your squirty lizard-goggles were awesome!"

TODAY'S MENU

YOUR CHOICE:

Hot dog (all gone!)

Warm dog

Chilly dog (freezing-cold — not covered in chili)

Frosty dog (hot dog milkshake)

"Thanks!" said Rip.

"I just can't believe Dr. Tallow didn't give you an X for stinking up the whole classroom!" said Nikki. "I got one for *clapping* wrong!"

"You should try being a perfect student. Like me!" said Rip.

Nikki grumbled as she dumped the stink sauce all over her chilly dog.

Alexander cleared his throat. "I guess you *do* keep getting in trouble, Nikki," he said. "But, uh, maybe Dr. Tallow will go easier on you tomorrow — after she sees your animal report."

"Yeah, maybe," said Nikki.

"Hey, Nikki! What kind of cupcakes do you like?" Dottie asked. "I'm bringing some to school next week for my birthday!"

Alexander could tell Dottie was trying to cheer Nikki up. It was sort of working.

"Strawberry," Nikki said with a tiny smile.

Alexander took a bite of his warm dog, which was now a chilly dog.

He leaned over to grab a mustard bottle from the next table. But he couldn't quite reach it . . .

CRINKLE! Someone wearing strange, shiny clothes handed the mustard bottle to Alexander.

"Thanks for — !" Alexander gasped, almost choking on his chilly dog.

The tall, shiny figure at the next table wasn't a person at all. It was an angry monster, covered in bubble wrap!

CHAPTER 6 BLOWN AWAY

"A*aah!*" Alexander yelped. He fell out of his seat, squeezing mustard all over himself. "Run! It's the bumpy mummy!"

BUMPY MUMMY
Bubble-wrap
warrior

"What are you talking about?" asked Nikki, helping Alexander to his feet. "We flattened that monster *ages* ago."

"You just saw a monster?" asked Dottie. "Was it one of those snow-zombies?"

"They're called *snombies*, Dottie," said Rip. "And no, Salamander didn't see a monster."

Alexander wiped his face on his sleeve. His eyes stung from the mustard.

"I *did* see one!" yelled Alexander. "If it wasn't a monster, then who passed me the mustard?!" He pointed over his shoulder.

There was no one at the next table.

"Why are you shouting, Alexander?" asked Dr. Tallow, rushing over. "Oh, my! You're covered in mustard!"

"I'm fine," Alexander said. "I just, uh, really like mustard."

Dr. Tallow turned to Rip. "Dearie, could you help Alexander get cleaned up?" she asked.

"Sure thing!" said Rip.

"I'll clean this mustard off his chair and backpack," said Dr. Tallow.

"No!" said Nikki.

Dr. Tallow raised an eyebrow.

"I mean, *we'll* clean his backpack," said Nikki, grabbing Dottie's arm.

"Come on, mustard-pants," said Rip. He dragged Alexander to the bathroom.

Like the rest of their new school, everything in the bathroom was high-tech.

Alexander splashed water on his face.

"Rip, *what* is happening?" he asked. "First I see a balloon goon, and now a bumpy mummy!"

"Salamander, you're seeing things," Rip said, frowning. "We already battled those monsters! You must've stayed up too late last night."

"Maybe you're right," said Alexander.
He walked to the hand-dryer on the wall.

Alexander hit the middle button.

VWOOORRRRRR! A gust of oven-hot air blasted Alexander. He was dry in two seconds.

"Whoa!" he said. "That dryer could cook a turkey!"

Rip snorted.

BRINNNGGGG!!

"Recess!" said Rip, kicking open the door. "Come on, weenie! We're wasting valuable play time!"

7 NOT IT!

Nikki and Dottie were waiting for Alexander and Rip on the playground.

"Catch, Salamander!" said Nikki. She tossed Alexander his backpack.

Alexander looked it over. "Thanks for cleaning off the mustard," he said.

Nikki leaned in. "You've got to be more careful! You keep the *notebook* in there," she whispered. "Remember how the last monster we battled said that a boss-monster was after the notebook?"

Alexander nodded. "Good call, Nikki," he said.

33

"So . . . how about some freeze tag?" Dottie suggested.

"Yeah!" said Rip. He pointed to Nikki. "You're IT!"

Nikki smiled and began chasing her friends.

She tagged Alexander right away. He froze in place.

Then he watched Rip escape from Nikki on the monkey bars.

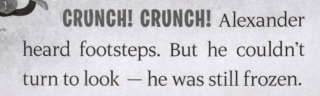

CRUNCH! CRUNCH! Alexander heard footsteps. But he couldn't turn to look — he was still frozen.

WHAP! Something smacked his shoulder.

"Hey!" he said, turning around. "Don't tag me so — **BWAH!**" Alexander yelped.

He was nose-to-nose with a giant, growling carrot.

MEAT-EATING VEGETABLE
Hungry for juicy grade-schoolers

"Alexander?!" Dottie called out from behind the swings.

The carrot dashed off and jumped into a rocket-shaped playhouse.

Dottie rushed over. "What *was* that thing?" she cried. "I'm going to find out!"

"Dottie, careful!" Alexander shouted as she darted inside the playhouse.

Nikki and Rip ran over when they saw the look on Alexander's face.

"I saw a veggie monster!" Alexander said.

Nikki gave Rip a look.

"I'm serious!" said Alexander.

"That big orange thing ran off!" Dottie said, catching her breath. "I couldn't get a good look."

Alexander sighed. "Thanks for trying, Dottie."

"Geez, Salamander," said Rip. "A balloon goon, a mummy, and now a veggie?"

"I know — it sounds crazy," Alexander said.

"Yeah," agreed Nikki. "How could three of the monsters we've beaten come back?"

"Well . . ." said Alexander, "maybe *another* monster is bringing them back . . ."

He pulled out the notebook.

MMMM! Violet fungus smells like peppermint.

BEHAVIOR These tiny purple mushrooms sprout on the heads of clobbered monsters, bringing them back to life.

DIET Old, rotten monster parts. Also: grape soda.

WARNING! A monster controlled by violet fungus is twice as strong, and half as nice, as a regular monster!

"See? The violet fungus could be bringing back old monsters," said Alexander.

"So we should keep an eye out for minty purple mushrooms, right?" asked Dottie.

"You're a real pro, Dottie!" said Rip, winking.

"Thanks . . . I think?" said Dottie.

The members of the S.S.M.P. smiled at one another.

"Hey, Dottie, could you meet us after school today?" Alexander asked.

"Sure! Why?" said Dottie.

"We have something super secret to ask you!" said Nikki.

CHAPTER 8 THE FOURTH MEMBER

T he bunnies must love it here!" said Dottie, hopping over a log.

Alexander, Rip, and Nikki laughed. School had ended, and they were leading Dottie through the woods.

"Okay, here we are!" said Rip.

Dottie's eyes grew wide. "A caboose?" she said.

"Yep!" said Nikki. "It's our hideout!"

Dottie followed her friends into the caboose.

"Welcome to the Super Secret Monster Patrol headquarters!" said Alexander.

"This is where we keep our monster-fighting weapons," said Rip, swinging a ski pole like a sword.

"And here's our trunk of disguises," said Santa Claus. Actually, it wasn't Santa. It was Nikki in a fake beard and a hat.

"And here is our most important tool," said Alexander. He showed the notebook to Dottie. "It describes every monster in Stermont."

"But there's some kind of boss-monster out there trying to steal it," added Nikki.

"A boss-monster?!" said Dottie. "That sounds scary. How can I help?"

"Well . . ." said Alexander. "Rip, Nikki, and I think you'd make a perfect member of the S.S.M.P. Will you join us?"

Dottie's smile was bigger than the rabbit ears on her shirt. "Heck, yeah!" she said.

"Great!" said Alexander. "Then repeat after me." He flipped the notebook to the very first page and began to read.

When googly-eyed monsters all covered in ooze start swallowing school children whole,

I swear that I'll fight 'em (and try not to lose) by joining this secret patrol.

Dottie said the oath and became the fourth member of the S.S.M.P.

"Yay!" shouted Nikki.

"Fist bump!" shouted Rip.

"Look out!" shouted Alexander.

A long-eared shadow darted along the wall. Alexander jumped back, crashing into a shelf. **KER-BLONK!** Junk spilled everywhere.

"It's a shadow-smasher!" Alexander yelled.

SHADOW-SMASHER
Living darkness

"That's not a shadow-smasher!" Rip shouted.

Alexander looked again. The long-eared thing was Dottie's regular shadow, with her bunny backpack.

"Yikes, Salamander," said Nikki. "I thought you were onto something with the violet fungus, but now you're jumping at shadows!"

"Just go home and get some rest," said Rip.

"Don't worry, we'll pick up all of this stuff," added Dottie.

"Okay, thanks guys," he said.

Alexander trudged home.

9 SNOW FOOLIN'

Alexander kept an eye out for monsters as he rode to school the next morning.

He parked his bike, and glanced back at the hedge where he had seen the goon yesterday.

RUSTLE RUSTLE! Something moved!

Alexander ran over. He dropped to his hands and knees, and peered into the hedge. Just some rocks, a paper cup, and a broken stick.

RUSTLE! The stick wiggled.

Alexander gasped. That was no ordinary stick — it was an arm! The arm of a snombie!

SNOMBIE
Throws kid-freezing
snowballs

RUSTLE-RUSTLE-CRUNCH! A giant snombie rose from the hedge.

We melted the snombies last summer, thought Alexander. *I know we did! This must be the work of the violet fungus!*

He squinted — looking for tiny purple mushrooms on the snombie's head. But there were none.

Alexander braced himself for the icy **SPLAT** of a snowball.

But instead of walloping Alexander, the big snombie rolled behind the building.

Alexander was no longer afraid. He was angry. "Get back here, snombie!" he shouted.

CLACK! The back door swung shut.

The monster must have run inside! thought Alexander.

Alexander ran through the door, into a dark hallway. There was an elevator at the end of the hall, and its doors were closing. The snombie stood inside.

"Stop!" Alexander shouted. He dashed to the elevator. He stuck his arm through the doors, touching the snombie's belly. He expected his hand to freeze from the cold. But instead, the snombie felt warm and smooshy.

"Gross!" Alexander shouted, jumping back. The elevator doors slid closed.

The indicator on the wall showed the elevator going up to the ninth floor.

My classroom's up there! he thought. *My friends could be in danger!*

Alexander hit the UP button.

What kind of monster is warm and smooshy? he thought. He flipped through the notebook while he waited for the elevator.

MEANBAG

Comfy seat that likes to eat.

DIET You!

BEHAVIOR Meanbags don't mind being sat on, as long as you're watching cartoons.

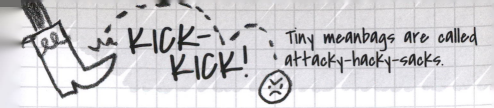

KICK-KICK!

Tiny meanbags are called attacky-hacky-sacks.

HABITAT In front of the TV.

WARNING! These guys hate commercials! As soon as an ad comes on: CHOMP-CHOMP-GULP!

BING! The elevator was back. But the doors didn't open. Alexander pressed the UP button again. Nothing happened.

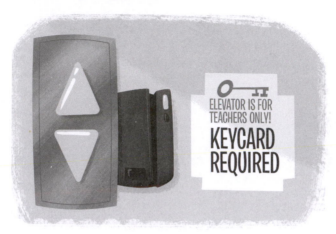

Rats! thought Alexander. *I have to get up there!*

He ran back outside, then into the lobby, up the escalators, around the corner and—

KER-BLASH!

He plowed right into Dr. Tallow, knocking her to the ground.

10 CRASH COURSE

Sorry, Dr. Tallow!" said Alexander. "Are you all right?"

Dr. Tallow's glasses were off-kilter. "Help me up, dearie!"

Alexander helped steady his teacher as she got to her feet. Her hand felt dry. "Now, why on Earth were you running so fast?" she asked.

Alexander gulped. Then he spoke, quietly.

"Um, er . . . did you see a . . ." he began.

Dr. Tallow straightened her glasses, and peered over them at Alexander. "A *what*, dearie?" she asked.

"Um . . ." Alexander swallowed. "A snowman?"

Dr. Tallow laughed. But then she noticed Alexander was not laughing.

"No," she said. "No snowmen up here—just me."

Alexander gave her a weak smile.

"You seem jumpy today," Dr. Tallow said. "And yesterday, too, come to think of it." She rubbed lotion on her hands.

"Oh, I'm fine," Alexander said.

"I know it can be hard to ask for help," said Dr. Tallow. "But please know that I'm here if you need me."

She squatted down to look in Alexander's eyes. "Actually, I was hoping to ask *you* for help."

"Me?" said Alexander.

"Yes," Dr. Tallow said. "I'm afraid your friend Nikki doesn't like me. Could you try talking to her?"

"I guess so," said Alexander.

BRINNGG!

Dr. Tallow smiled. "It looks like we're both late again," she said. "Come on, let's get to class."

11 THE LAST STRIKE

Alexander followed Dr. Tallow into the classroom. Students were once again standing around, yakking.

Dr. Tallow picked up a stack of notecards. "Alexander, why don't you have a word with Nikki while I pass these out?" she suggested.

Alexander walked over to Nikki.

"Salamander!" said Nikki. "Where have you been?"

"I was outside—chasing a snombie!" said Alexander.

"Were there mushrooms on its head?" asked Nikki. "Or did the monster somehow vanish, like the others?"

"No mushrooms—I checked," said Alexander. "And the snombie didn't vanish. It took the elevator!" He paused. "Can I ask you something?"

"Yeah, sure," Nikki said.

"Could you, uh, try being a little nicer to Dr. Tallow?" asked Alexander. "She thinks you don't like her."

"I can't believe you're taking her side!" Nikki said. "I'm trying my best! She just doesn't like *me*!"

Rip ran up, waving a notecard. "Look! Dr. Tallow loves me! She gave me a note saying we're BFFs!"

Nikki rolled her eyes. "That's not a note! It's your grade," she said.

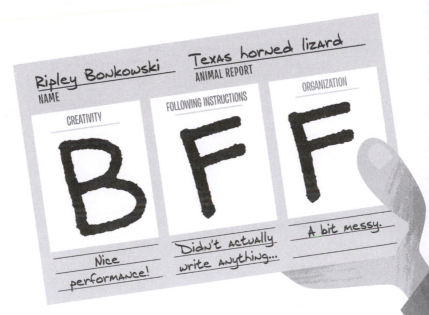

Ripley Bonkowski
NAME

Texas horned lizard
ANIMAL REPORT

CREATIVITY

FOLLOWING INSTRUCTIONS

ORGANIZATION

B F F

Nice performance!

Didn't actually write anything...

A bit messy.

"Yeah, yeah," said Rip. "Let's see how you do on *your* project!" He stomped back to his seat.

CLAP! CLAP! CLAP-CLAP-CLAP!

"To your seats, dearies," Dr. Tallow sang. "It's time for Nikki's animal report."

She gave Nikki an ear-to-ear smile.

Nikki picked up a fishbowl from her desk and walked to the front of the room.

She cleared her throat and began to speak. "Goldfish make great pets—"

"Louder, dear!" Dr. Tallow interrupted.

Nikki gritted her teeth, and spoke louder. "Goldfish can also—"

"Stand up straight, please!" said Dr. Tallow.

Nikki unslouched her shoulders. The fishbowl jiggled, splashing a drop of water onto the carpet.

"Oh no. You've made a mess," said Dr. Tallow.

Nikki's hand was shaking as she pointed to Rip's stink-blaster on the bookcase. "Rip stinks up the whole room, and he's your BFF!" she yelled. "But I spill one drop of water and *I'm* making a mess?!"

Everyone gasped.

Dr. Tallow silently walked to the board.

"Last strike, missy," she said. Dr. Tallow added a twentieth X after Nikki's name.

TWENTY STRIKES AND YOU'RE OUT!

NIKKI: xxxxx xxxxx xxxxx xxxxx

RIP: x

Then she pressed the intercom button and said, "Please send Ms. Vanderpants, right away."

Nikki stood in silence. The class sat in silence. The goldfish swam in silence.

A minute later, the door opened. Principal Vanderpants entered the room.

Dr. Tallow pointed to Nikki.

"Come with me," said Ms. Vanderpants.

Nikki's shoulders slumped. She frowned at Alexander, and then followed the principal out of the room.

CHAPTER 12 BLAH BLAH BLOB

"I can't believe Nikki got in trouble," said Dottie, putting on her backpack.

"Yeah," Rip said. "A whole day in Vanderpants's office . . ."

"Maybe we're wrong about Dr. Tallow," said Alexander. "Maybe she *isn't* being fair to Nikki."

"No way!" Rip said. "Tallow rules!"

"Let's just find Nikki so we can walk home," said Dottie.

"You guys go get Nikki and meet me back here," Alexander said. "I need to ask Dr. Tallow something."

Dr. Tallow was in the classroom-pet zone. Alexander walked inside.

"Uh, excuse me," said Alexander.

Dr. Tallow dropped a cucumber slice into the hamster cage.

"Yes, dearie?" she said, without looking up.

"Well, it's about Nikki," said Alexander. "I think maybe you were too hard on her."

Dr. Tallow stroked the hamster's back. Then she looked at Alexander. She was frowning.

"You're right," she said. "I should apologize."

Alexander blinked in surprise.

"I've been stressed lately, and I'm taking it out on Nikki," said Dr. Tallow. "And the reason I'm so stressed is—oh, you wouldn't believe me."

Dr. Tallow sniffled. Her eyes filled with tears. Alexander wasn't used to seeing grown-ups get upset. "Uh, it's okay," he mumbled.

"I have a secret that I cannot tell anyone. Especially other grown-ups—they'd never believe me," said Dr. Tallow. "But you, Alexander . . . I hope *you* will believe me. I've been seeing . . . monsters! All over Stermont!"

Alexander's mouth fell open.

"First I saw a tall, wiggly balloon creature," Dr. Tallow continued. "Then I saw a mummy and a giant carrot."

"I believe you!" cried Alexander.

He dropped his voice to a whisper. "And I can help you. I'm a member of the Super Secret Monster Patrol. We fight monsters—with this!"

He pulled the notebook from his backpack.

Dr. Tallow's eyes grew extra-extra-extra wide. "May I see that?" she asked, reaching for the notebook.

Nikki burst into the room, with Rip and Dottie in tow. She snatched the notebook from Alexander's hand.

"I've told you before!" Nikki shouted. "You need to be *careful* with this!"

Dr. Tallow dropped her cucumbers and turned to Nikki. "You foolish jampire! *Good* monsters are the worst!" she yelled. Her face turned bright pink. "My boss wants that book! I must have it NOW!"

"Huh?!" said Alexander, taking a step back.

"Alexander, if I had to grade you on monster-fighting, I'd give you straight Fs," said Dr. Tallow. Her face twisted into an angry scowl. "You've overlooked the one monster who's been in front of you for months . . ."

Dr. Tallow's face drooped. Her arms wobbled. She melted into a blob of pink goo, with mean, yellow eyes.

CHAPTER 13 QUITE A STRETCH

Noooooo!" Rip cried. "My favorite teacher is a *blob?*"

"I'm no ordinary blob, dearie," said the pink ooze. "I'm the shape-shifting super-goop! I can take any form!"

68

VLOOP! The blob twisted around, making a sound like a boot being pulled from thick mud. An instant later, it had molded itself into a new shape—a balloon goon. Then—**VLOOP!**—a mummy, a carrot, a snombie, and back to a blob.

Alexander gasped. "Those monsters I saw—they were all *you*!"

"Yes, I turned into those monsters when you were alone," said the blob. "I knew none of these dum-dums would believe you!"

"Salamander really *did* see those monsters!" said Rip.

"One monster, Rip—a Silly Putty monster!" said Dottie.

The super-goop extended a pink, rubbery arm toward Nikki. Nikki clutched the notebook to her chest as the super-goop's arm clamped down around her shoulders.

"Now give me that notebook!" the monster yelled.

"Never!" said Nikki. She tossed the notebook to Alexander. He zipped it into his backpack.

VLOOP! Two more arms shot out, wrapping around Alexander and Dottie like vines.

The hamsters, turtles, and fish hid in their tunnels, shells, and plastic castles.

Rip took a step back, toward the doorway.

VLOOP! Dr. Tallow's pink, smiling face appeared on the blob. "Rip, dearie, there's no need to run," she said. "You and I are alike!"

"Alike?!" yelled Rip. "I'm not a mon—"

CHOMP! Nikki bit the super-goop's arm.

"Ouch!" the blob shouted. Alexander felt the monster loosen its grip.

"Rip, catch!" Alexander yelled. He flung his backpack to Rip. "RUN! Don't let her get the notebook!"

Rip darted out the door.

The Tallow-faced blob followed him, locking the door behind her.

"We're trapped!" said Nikki.

Alexander, Nikki, and Dottie could hear Rip shouting from the other side of the door. But they couldn't understand what he was saying.

"Rip needs us!" said Nikki. "We've got to get out of here!"

"No problem," said Dottie. "I saw Dr. Tallow enter the code yesterday."

Dottie walked over to the keypad and pressed a few buttons. **BOOP!** The door swung open.

Alexander smiled. "Dottie, I'm *so* glad you're in the S.S.M.P.!" he said.

Alexander, Nikki, and Dottie ran into the classroom.

Two boys were having a tug-of-war over Alexander's backpack. They both wore black shirts. They both had square heads.

They were both Rip Bonkowski.

CHAPTER 14 OOZE THE NEW GUY?

The two Rips growled at each other as they jerked on the backpack.

"Guys!" shouted Rip-1. "That squishy glop of super-goop changed itself to look like me!"

"Don't believe that phony!" said Rip-2. "*I'm* the real Rip!"

The two Rips were punching, kicking, and fighting dirty—like only a Rip could do.

Alexander, Nikki, and Dottie watched from the back of the room.

"What do we do?" asked Nikki.

"We blast the fake Rip," said Alexander. He grabbed Rip's stink-blaster, and strapped it on.

"Stop or I'll squirt!" he shouted.

Both Rips froze, mid-punch. They were each holding one strap of Alexander's backpack.

"Blast him! Not me!" they said at once.

Alexander looked back at Nikki and Dottie.

"Ask a question that only the *real* Rip could answer," suggested Dottie.

"What does S.S.M.P. stand for?" asked Nikki, stepping forward.

"Super Secret Monster Patrol," said both Rips.

"That won't work," Alexander said. "I, um, told Dr. Tallow about the S.S.M.P."

"You *what*?!" said Nikki.

"Blast that other Rip already!" said Rip-1. "He's clearly a weenie!"

"Don't blast *me*, Salamander!" yelled Rip-2. "You're my very best friend in the whole world!"

"Aha!" said Alexander. "The *real* Rip would never say something so sappy." He squeezed the trigger on the stink-blaster.

Rip-2 let go of the backpack to block his face as Alexander soaked him with stink sauce.

"Thanks, dearie!" yelled Rip-1, yanking the backpack away. "Time for me to bounce!"

Alexander, Nikki, and Dottie gasped.

VLOOP! Rip-1 melted into a gooey blob and shot out of the classroom. It was wearing Alexander's backpack!

15 COOK WHO'S TALKING

Yeesh," said the real Rip, sopping wet with stink-sauce. "That was the first and last time I say something nice!"

"Sorry," said Alexander as he helped Rip to his feet.

"Come on!" shouted Nikki from the door. "The monster's getting away!"

The four of them ran into the hallway. The super-goop was near the escalators.

"You can't catch me!" the monster shouted.

VLOOP! The super-goop morphed into a giant rabbit, and hopped down the steps.

"Oh no!" said Dottie.
"Bunnies are super fast!"
"Even on escalators?" said Rip.
THUMP!-THUMP!-THUMP! They chased the rabbit down the steps and caught up with it on the next floor down. But just as Alexander reached out to grab the backpack . . .

VLOOP! The super-
goop became a salamander,
running along the wall.

"**BWUK-HYUK-HYUK!**"
laughed the monster. "I'm using
your own animal reports against you!"

VLOOP! It snapped back
into blob-form, and oozed
down to the second floor.

"It's heading into the
cafeteria!" shouted Nikki.

"Follow that blob!" said
Alexander. "We've got to
get the notebook!"

By the time they got downstairs, the cafeteria
was empty.

"Through those doors, maybe?" asked Rip.

They walked into the kitchen. It was dark. And warm.

"It smells yummy in here," said Dottie. Loaves of bread were cooling near two giant ovens.

SLAM! The kitchen doors burst open, and the rubbery pink blob bounced in.

"Did you miss me?" said the monster.

VLOOP. Four noodly arms shot out, wrapping around each member of the monster patrol.

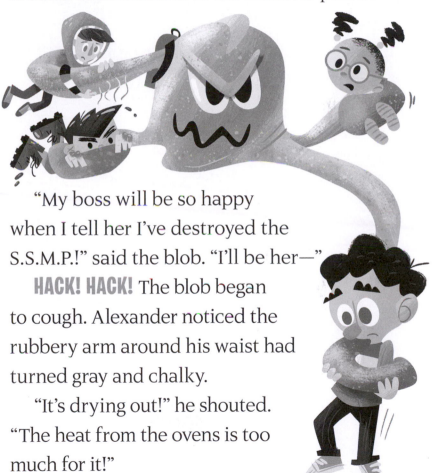

"My boss will be so happy when I tell her I've destroyed the S.S.M.P.!" said the blob. "I'll be her—"

HACK! HACK! The blob began to cough. Alexander noticed the rubbery arm around his waist had turned gray and chalky.

"It's drying out!" he shouted. "The heat from the ovens is too much for it!"

HACK! The super-goop began to crack and crumble. It released its grip on the four monster-fighters.

"It needs moisture!" said Nikki.

"That's why Dr. Tallow was always using lotion!" said Rip.

VLOOP! The crumbling blob turned into a pink goldfish. It flopped across the room and into a pot of water.

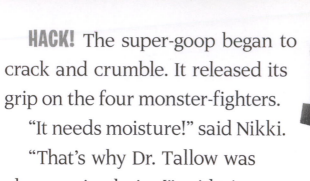

SPLOOSH!

Then the super-goop shot out of the water. It was no longer a goldfish. The monster was now a giant rubbery ball—large enough to flatten four kids in one bounce.

16 NO BOOK OF DOOM

BATHROOM

The S.S.M.P. ran back into the cafeteria. They weaved between lunch tables.

The super-goop rolled after them, bouncing off tables like a runaway boulder.

"Make a break for the bathroom!" Rip shouted.

The friends dashed into the bathroom.

SPROING! The monster barreled through the bathroom door.

Alexander, Nikki, and Dottie were huddled together.

"Hmmm . . . Where's Rip? I guess I'll deal with you three first," said the super-goop. "I know just what animal will finish you off!"

VLOOP! The super-goop transformed into a huge spiky creature. It began to puff itself up, nearly filling the bathroom.

Alexander gasped. *The Texas horned lizard!*

"Prepare to be poked!" shouted the monster. "And then squished!"

KER-CLACK!

Rip kicked open a stall. "Hot enough for ya, goop-for-brains?" he shouted.

BAM! He hit the SAHARA DESERT button on the hand-dryer.

VWOOORRRRRR

DRY
SUPER DRY
SAHARA DESERT

A hot, dry whirlwind swirled around the room. "Uh-oh," said the super-goop. Then—**CRICK!**— the monster became instantly dry and hard.

"Nice work, Rip!" Alexander said. He snatched his backpack from one of the creature's spikes.

"Is someone playing in there?!" shouted an angry voice.

Ms. Vanderpants marched into the bathroom. Her eyes narrowed as she looked around the room.

Broken door

Giant weird spiky statue

Stinky, drippy Rip

Kids in the school, after hours

"You four. Out. Now," she said.

The S.S.M.P. left their grumbling principal in the bathroom.

"That was weird," said Dottie.

"Yeah," said Rip. "Super weird."

"Ms. Vanderpants didn't yell at us," said Dottie.

"And she didn't ask about the giant baked super-goop," added Alexander.

"You know, Ms. Vanderpants *was* acting weird when I was in her office today," said Nikki. "She kept carrying big white buckets into the hall."

"What was in the buckets?" asked Dottie.

"Not sure," said Nikki. "But anyway, I'd take strange Principal Vanderpants over that jampire-hater Dr. Tallow any day."

"Yeah, yeah," said Rip. "You were right about her."

Alexander reached into his backpack for the notebook.

"Uh . . . Guys?" he said. He shook his backpack upside down.

A note fell out.

Everyone froze. The notebook was gone.

Alexander's stomach felt queasy, and it wasn't from the stink sauce.

"What's the note say?" asked Nikki.

Dear S.S.M.P.:
You may have gotten your backpack back.
But your notebook is with
the BOSS-MONSTER now!
Good luck fighting monsters without it!
        -SUPER-GOOP
            (AKA Dr. Tallow)

"Now what?" said Rip.

"Now we get our notebook back—even if it means going up against the boss-monster," said Alexander.

The S.S.M.P. sat quietly on the kitchen floor as Alexander turned over the note. He wrote a report about the super-goop.

SUPER-GOOP

Not-so-silly putty

HABITAT Stermont
Elementary School, ninth floor.

TROY CUMMINGS

has no tail, no wings, no fangs, no claws, and only one head. As a kid, he believed that monsters might really exist. Today, he's sure of it.

BEHAVIOR This creature tries to make silly putty animals, but they all end up looking like smooshed blobs.

HABITAT The wallyball court.

(Wallyball = volleyball x racquetball. Picture a bunch of old guys and a big rubber ball bouncing off the walls until they all go home, deflated.)

DIET Strawberry banana smoothies.

EVIDENCE Few people believe that Troy Cummings is real. The only proof we have is that he supposedly wrote and illustrated The Eensy-Weensy Spider Freaks Out!, and Giddy-up, Daddy!

WARNING Keep your eyes peeled for more danger in The Notebook of Doom #11:

SNEEZE OF THE OCTO-SCHNOZZ

THE NOTEBOOK OF DOOM

QUESTIONS & ACTIVITIES!

Why was Dottie invited to join the S.S.M.P.? Do you think she will be a good monster fighter? Why or why not?

What **clues** hinted at Dr. Tallow's true identity? Reread if necessary.

How does the super-goop use information from the S.S.M.P.'s animal reports against them?

Do the members of the S.S.M.P. defeat the super-goop? Explain your answer.

Animals are awesome! Work with a partner to research an animal. Create a report similar to Alexander's on page 2. Be sure to add true and exciting facts about the animal!